Musician's I
of Wis

By Scott E. Power

ICS BOOKS, Inc.
Merrillville, IN

Musician's Little Book of Wisdom

Published by:
ICS BOOKS, Inc.
1370 E. 86th Place
Merrillville, IN 46410
800-541-7323

Printed in the U.S.A.

Cover illustration by
Demetrius Saulsberry

Co-Published in Canada by:
Vanwell Publishing LTD
1 Northrup Crescent
St. Catharines, Ontario
L2M 6P5
800-661-6136

Library of Congress Cataloging-in-Publication Data

Power, Scott E. , 1970-
       Musician's little book of wisdom / by Scott Power.
            p.   cm.
       ISBN 1-57034-048-X
       1. Music--Quotations, maxims, etc.   I Title.
       PN6084 . M8P68   1996   96-22582
       780--dc20   CIP

Dedication

This book is dedicated to those people who taught me to love music: My wonderful family and music instructors Troy Neihardt, Ellen Pierce, George Porumb, Bob Symer, Ray Garvetti, Joe Stevens, and Frank Collier. Thank you for showing me how music enriches our lives and keeps us singing. Music is one of life's greatest gifts. God bless you all.

Acknowledgements

I would like to acknowledge all of those who made this book possible: Funnster Tom Todd and his crew at ICS Books, Inc., for publishing the book; special thanks to William W. Forgey, M.D., Troy Neihardt, Dave Roberts, and Frank Collier for their editorial talents. Their input makes this book worth reading.

Introduction

If you consider yourself a musician, this book is for you. Whether you play guitar in a rock band or on the porch swing, play cello for the Chicago Symphony Orchestra or *Chop Sticks* on the piano. If you sing in a choir or in the shower, get paid to perform or just love listening to music, *Musician's Little Book of Wisdom* is for you. Within these pages you can read Mozart, Beethoven, and Miles Davis talking about music, being a musician and what they have learned along the way. Hear from contemporary, non-famous, working musicians, as well as popular artists such as Billy Joel, Pete Townshend, and John Lennon.

Musician's Little Book of Wisdom is filled with four hundred and forty bits of wisdom created the only way wisdom can be—through experience. You may have heard the axiom "Hindsight is 20/20." It is. However, there's a problem. You have to make a mistake first before you achieve the wisdom of hindsight.

• MUSICIAN'S LITTLE BOOK OF WISDOM •

The advantage of experience is empowerment to recognize the same mistake every time you make it. But what if you could talk to or ask questions of someone like Beethoven, Copland, Ellington, or Hendrix? Just sit down face-to-face, talk heart-to heart, and get advice that you would otherwise have to learn the hard way. *Musician's Little Book of Wisdom* is that sort of reference tool.

If you're a musician and want to be the best you can be, read this book. If you know a musician, pass it along to your friend. Don't just stand there. Get strumming.

Scott Power
Bachelor of Liberal Arts, Music Business,
Columbia College, Chicago.

1. In the beginning was rhythm.

2. "Without music, life would be an error."
   — Friedrich Nietzsche

3. "Always treat fellow musicians with respect,
   regardless of talent."
   — Troy Neihardt, Chicago musician

4. Never judge musicians by the size of their
   instruments.

5. Never judge musicians by the length of their hair.

6. Learn as much as you can as fast as you can.

7. Knowledge is fuel for self–improvement.

8. "Imagination is more important than knowledge."
    — Einstein

9. "Music produces a kind of pleasure which human nature cannot do without."
— Confucius

10. "The life of man in every part has need of harmony and rhythm."
— Plato

11. Always be open to the suggestions of other musicians.

12. The use of foresight when reading sheet music is helpful. It's helpful in everyday life too.

13. "It's only rock 'n' roll, but I like it."
— The Rolling Stones

14. Nowadays, the music business is more business than music.

15. Learn how the music business works.

16. "Because of the business I get to do the music."
— Melissa Etheridge, *Musician Magazine* (April 1995)

17. Subscribe to *Billboard Magazine*. It's the music biz trade journal.

18. Practice your business savvy along with your performance savvy.

19. Never pass up an opportunity to play live.

20. Everyone should learn to sing or play an instrument.

21. "Only a fool sold more of his time than he had to."
— Thoreau

22. Never feel obligated to perform an encore. Applause is a receipt, not a bill.

23. "When performing always let them see you sweat."
— Paul Westerberg,
Musician Magazine (April 1995)

24. Break a leg.

25. Not yours. *Theirs.*

26. A great song is a great song, but it is up to <u>you</u> to write that great song.

27. There's a lot of music biz jargon that musicians must understand and use to communicate with colleagues and management.

28. As soon as you write a song down, record it, or "fix" it in some fashion, so a copyright exists.

29. Once you have written a song, you have the exclusive right to reproduce copies of that song.

30. "When singing, always sing from your diaphragm. Not *that* diaphragm."
     — Dave Roberts, Chicago musician

31. Never let anyone tell you what to do.

32. When on tour, don't get caught trying to smuggle drugs.

33. Failure to properly affix the copyright notice on a work cannot cause that work to enter the public domain.

34.   Song titles are not protected by copyright law.

35.   For anyone to infringe on your copyright, you have to prove they had "access" to the copyrighted material.

36.   Keep track of whoever you send your demo tapes to. Without proof that someone had access to your song, you can't prove it was copied.

37.   One of the greatest compliments anyone
       could give you is to steal your material.

38.   A *"poor man's copyright"* (sending yourself
       a copy in the mail) will not hold up in a
       court of law.

39. Every serious musician should get a complete copy of the Copyright Act and other important published material relating to copyright. Get the materials for free from the Register of Copyrights, Copyright Office, Library of Congress, Washington, D.C. 20559.

40. There is a great deal of money to be made in music publishing and your knowledge of how that money is made will give you the chance to see that more of it goes into your pocket rather than someone else's.

41.   Once your period of greatest success is
       behind you, your income is subject to the
       agreements you signed at the time.

42.   You, as a songwriter, can and should make at
       least as much money on your songs as your
       publisher does.

43.   "If I had only known then what I know now,
       I wouldn't have signed that first contract
       without considering all of my options."
       — Every Songwriter That Ever Lived

44. Happiness comes when your work and words are of benefit to yourself and others.

45. "The artist should love life and show us that it is beautiful; without him, we might doubt."
— Gabriel Faure,
quoted in Mellers, *Studies In Contemporary Music* (1947)

46. "We have no art. We do everything as well as possible."
— Balinese musician

47. "There should be a single Art Exchange in the world, to which the artist would simply send his works and be given in return as much as he needs. As it is, one has to be half a merchant on top of everything else, and how badly one goes about it!"
— Beethoven

48. "I didn't do it!"
— The Liar

49.   "Once you give up your integrity, everything
      else is a piece of cake."
      — J.R. Ewing (TV's "Dallas")

50.   Treat people well on your way up. You may
      see them again on your way down.

51.   Forsake your honor amongst thieves and
      you'll run for the rest of your days.

52.   "Management, too, is an art."
      — Mozart's father...and manager.

53. If anyone gives you criticism that starts off with "you should" or "you shouldn't," walk away immediately.

54. "We don't play to be seen. I'm addicted to the music, not audiences."
— Miles Davis

55. "The one thing I hate at the Met is the note in the programme that the public is requested not to interrupt the music with applause."
— Placido Domingo

56. "I know two kinds of audience only—
     one coughing and one not coughing."
     — Arthur Schnabel

57. "I never understood the need for a 'live'
     audience. My music, because of its extreme
     quietude, would be happiest with a
     dead one."
     — Igor Stravinsky

58. "If you need your family and friends to come down and see you perform, you're no performer."
    — Paul Westerberg,
    Musician Magazine (April 1995)

59. "The ultimate good is not to be afraid."
    — Nietzsche

60. "It's not about production. It's about the immediacy of the music and lyrics."
    — Bonnie Raitt,
    Musician Magazine (April 1995)

61. "It is often by seeing and hearing musical works (operas and other good musical compositions), rather than by rules, that taste is formed."
— Jean–Philippe Rameau,
Le Nouveau Systeme De Musique Theorique
(1725)

62. "If an idea strikes me as beautiful and satisfactory to the ear and heart, I would far rather overlook a grammatical error than sacrifice what is beautiful to mere pedantic trifling."
— Joseph Haydn,
quoted in Nohl, *Life of Haydn* (1883)

63. "Nothing is more futile than theorizing about music. No doubt there are laws, mathematically strict laws, but these laws are not music; they are only its conditions. The essence of music is revelation."
— Heinrich Heine, *Letters On The French Stage* (1837)

64. "Synchronization royalties" are monies earned by publishers for granting the right to use a song in a film or television show. There isn't a set rate. Publishers charge what they want to.

65. "Mechanical royalties" are monies paid by a record company for the right to manufacture and distribute recordings containing a song owned by the publisher.

66. "I would say to love what you do. On any level, love it; do it because you have to do it, because you want to do it. Do it for whoever you can, wherever you can and what happens beyond that is just icing on the cake."
    — Melissa Etheridge,
    Musician Magazine (April 1995)

67.   Enthusiasm is like a contact buzz. When you're around it, you feel it too.

68.   *Black's Law Dictionary* defines "breach of contract" as "failure, without legal excuse, to perform any promise which forms the whole or part of a contract."

69.   The amount of income that can be made from the use of a song in a commercial is substantial.

70. A lot of songwriters have clauses in their publishing contracts that allow the writer the final decision about whether or not his song will be used to advertise a product or service, as well as the manner in which the song will be used.

71. Some songs are so historical and/or socially important that publishers will not let any advertiser use them.

72.   "Residuals" are payments to singers and musicians for subsequent use of a performance in an advertisement or on television.

73.   Above all else, persevere.

74.   "A musicologist is a man who can read music but can't hear it."
       — Sir Thomas Beecham, quoted in Atkins and Newman, *Beecham Stories* (1978)

75. Societies such as ASCAP, BMI, or SESAC do the legwork required to make sure both songwriters and music publishers are properly compensated for public performances of their music.

76. Licensees who pay fees to ASCAP, BMI, and SESAC are major television networks, radio stations, restaurants, hotels, concert halls, Musak, and the like.

77. Monk: "Where can I enter Zen?"
Master Gensha: "Can you hear the babbling brook?"
Monk: "Yes, I can hear it."
Master Gensha: "Then enter there."
— Master Gensha (831–908)

78. "To the dull mind, nature is leaden. To the illumined mind, the whole world burns and sparkles with light."
— Ralph Waldo Emerson

79.   "It is difficult to say whether accompanist or
       soloist deserves greater credit. Nevertheless,
       the soloist takes all the bravos to himself and
       gives no credit to his accompanist. But he is
       right, for he knows that ignorant custom
       directs these bravos to him alone."
       — Carl Philipp Emanuel Bach,
       *Essay On The True Art of Playing Keyboard
       Instruments*

80. "Even when alone, men comfort their
    weariness with song, however unskilled."
    — Quintilian,
    De Institutione Oratoria

81. "I want to know the thoughts of God. All the
    rest are details."
    — Einstein

82. An "Advance" is money paid to the songwriter or recording artist before regular royalty payment begins. Sometimes called "up front" money, advances are usually deducted from royalties.

83. "Artists need to have genuine human experience before they can effectively express human emotions."
— Billy Joel,
Musician Magazine (April 1995)

84. A "Booking Agent" is a person who solicits work and schedules performances for entertainers, usually for a percentage of the fee.

85. Hire a booking agent to find work for you so you can concentrate on your music.

86. "The future music of this country (America) must be founded on what are called the Negro melodies."
    — Antonin Dvorak

87. The blues isn't what you're singing; the blues is what you feel.

88. Not all hit songs are considered marketable as sheet music.

89. "If I knew then what I know now, I would have started out playing both the piano and the drums."
— Jimmy Health,
Musician Magazine (April 1995)

90. "You have to remember that the music
     comes first. That's why you get into this."
     — Dolores O'Riorder of The Cranberries,
     Musician Magazine (April 1995)

91. "The way to write American music is
     simple. All you have to do is be an
     American and then write any kind of music
     you wish."
     — Virgil Thomson, quoted in Machlis,
     Introduction To Contemporary Music (1963)

92. A hit song in the U.S. usually goes international as well, either by country–by–country subpublishing agreements or a single, worldwide subpublishing agreement.

93. The "Best Edition" of a work is published in the United States at any time before the date of deposit, that the Library of Congress determines to be the most suitable for its purposes.

94. "A merry heart doeth good like a medicine."
    — Proverbs 17:22

95. He who laughs lasts.

96. Even the slightest difference in the type of
    agreement you sign can mean a significant
    difference in royalties earned on a hit song.

97. "Before signing any documents, I would have sought the counsel of an attorney of my own choosing, independent of business managers, record companies, or anyone else with a vested interest in my financial future."
— Billy Joel,
Musician Magazine (April 1995)

98. A properly constructed agreement can protect both the writer and the publisher in any given situation.

99. An "A&R (Artists & Repertoire) Director" is a record company executive responsible for finding and developing new talent.

100. "Keep your nose clean and your chin up, even if it requires surgery."
— Ray Davies,
Musician Magazine (April 1995)

101. "Practice more than any band you know of. After that, practice some more."
— Henry Rollins,
Musician Magazine (April 1995)

102. "We hear too much music. Until we have a great listening public, and not just a passively hearing one, we will never be a musically cultured nation."
— Leonard Bernstein

103. "Of all the noises, I think music the least disagreeable."
— Samuel Johnson,
quoted in *The Morning Chronicle* (1816)

104. The Songwriters Guild of America offers
      three types of memberships: Associate
      Membership for unpublished writers;
      Regular Memberships for published writers;
      and Special Associate Membership for
      heirs of published songwriters. The SGA is
      located at 276 Fifth Ave., New York, NY
      10001. Call them at 212-686-6820.

105. A publisher's offer to advance money to
      the songwriter shows that the publisher is
      willing to gamble real cash to get the
      song recorded.

106. A "song shark" is anyone who demands money up front from a songwriter to promote the song.

107. Never do business with a song shark or with anyone who demands money up front for their services.

108. "We've gotten more success from that old thought of 'let's just get on the bus and go— and we'll worry about what we're gonna wear when we get there.'"
— Steven Tyler, *Aerosmith*

109. "MIDI" is an acronym for Musical Instrument Digital Interface.

110. A "split publishing agreement" divides publishing rights between two or more publishers.

111. "I can't listen to music too often. It affects my nerves."
— V.I. Lenin

112. With a "single song contract," there is sometimes a specified amount of time in which the publisher has to acquire a recording deal for the song. If the allotted time passes without a record deal, all rights revert back to the writer.

113. Attitude is a little thing that makes a big difference.

114. Don't confuse attitude with ego. An inflated ego can be a destructive thing.

115. "Pop music is ultimately a show, a circus.
You've got to hit the audience with it.
Punch them in the stomach, and kick them
on the floor."
— Pete Townshend

116. A staff writer's "contract term" is usually a
one–year term with a specific series of
one–year options.

117. As a staff writer, the publisher and writer usually agree on a set "quota" or number of acceptable songs the staff writer must produce each year.

118. "Never be frightened to take enough time to write."
— Mike Rutherford of Genesis

119. Some publishers argue that songs written by a staff writer are "works made for hire" and claim that copyright ownership belongs to the publisher under the copyright law.

120. Companies have no conscience. Realizing that is the first step in taking your future into your own hands.

121. A business cannot *feel*. It only cares about profitability.

122. "It does not matter how slowly you go as long as you do not stop."
— Confucius

123. The race is not always to the swift, but to those who keep running.

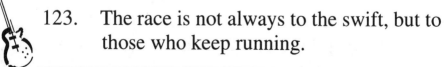

124. The quest for excellence never ends.

125. "When performing live, never throw anything at the audience that you don't want thrown back at you."
— Dave Roberts, Chicago musician

126. Make sure your music speaks for itself.

127. When soloing, play 75% on the inside and 25% on the outside. This will create tension, but not too much.

128. Remember that you are a professional and should conduct all business matters accordingly.

129. A musician listens to all styles of music.

130. No musician has the right to be self–righteous or elitist.

131. Just because some performers have fame and fortune necessarily doesn't mean they have talent.

132. "I have an audit done at least once every two years of my business manager's books and a professional review of investments made by that business manager."
— Billy Joel,
Musician Magazine (April 1995)

133. Never let your guard down.

134. Have a checklist of the gear you need to bring on tour. Otherwise you'll forget something.

135. Develop a mailing list at gigs by placing a pad of paper and pen by the sound board for people to sign. Fans enjoy getting stuff in the mail.

136. *Real* entertainers are born, not bred.

137. Stickers are inexpensive and make a fun advertising tool available to bands with limited budgets. Fans like them too.

138. When away from home on tour to play gigs, impose on friends, relatives, and cousins to house you.

139. When on tour and staying with others, cook for your hosts, always clean up after yourself, and don't forget to send a thank you after you leave.

140. Always remember to send postcards to your friends and family back home.

141.   When on a tour with a tight schedule, don't take the scenic route.

142.   Take the scenic route whenever possible.

143.   "Among all artists, travel is the least profitable for musicians. Our great composers have always dwelt quietly in one place and the same place: Bach, Haydn, Beethoven—although a view of the Alps or of Sicily might not have harmed them."
— Robert Schumann,
Collected Writings (1891)

144. "I didn't know composers had to take to the hills or the beach and talk with the muses for a few months to get a show."
— Duke Ellington

145. "All the inspiration I ever needed was a phone call from a producer."
— Cole Porter

146. "You're beautiful babe, never shave."
— The Music Biz Scoundrel

147.   Be cautious of anyone who calls you "babe."

148.   The tape recorder is the musician's mirror.
       Record yourself, listen and learn.

149.   "In order to be a great composer, one needs
       an enormous amount of knowledge, which
       one does not acquire from listening only to
       other people's work, but even more from
       listening to one's own."
       — Chopin

150. Most promoters will not pay in full prior to the performance. Always get half down before the gig and the balance during intermission. If they refuse to pay, refuse to play.

151. When planning a tour of college dates, call the college radio stations and ask what the hottest clubs are and what nights they are hot.

152. When on tour, get into town early to meet the locals and put them on your guest list. Someone may end up giving you a free roof over your head for the night.

153. Experience can be very costly. Don't be afraid to take a business class or two to help avoid mistakes.

154. Look for business courses that relate specifically to the music industry.

155. It is not our preferences that cause problems, but our attachment to them.

156. Just as beauty is in the eye of the beholder, music is in the ear of the listener.

157. "To have a lovely thought is nothing so remarkable. A thought comes of itself and if it is fine and great it is not our merit. But to carry out a thought well and make something great of it, that is the most difficult thing, that is, in fact – art!"
— Antonin Dvořák

158. "What distinguishes genius from talent is condensation."
— Einstein

159. "Genius is one percent inspiration, ninety–nine percent perspiration."
— Thomas Edison

160. Record companies don't know what good music is; they only know how to sell it as if it was good music.

161. The luckiest man in the world is the one who gets paid for doing what he loves.

162. Have foresight and think long-term. The short-term is just that: *short*.

163. Remember that no matter how famous you get, always respect mom and dad. They had to listen to you practice poorly all those years.

164. "The material of music is sound and silence.
Integrating these is composing."
— John Cage,
Silence (1961)

165. Always take your vitamins while on tour,
you'll need them.

166. Make sure the tour vehicle is stocked with
jumper cables, tools, a spare tire, gas, oil,
water, spark plugs, duct tape, flares, and a
"HELP" sign.

167. When merchandising t–shirts, buttons, stickers, and records, always display in clear view.

168. Price merchandise fairly. Don't be greedy.

169. You may qualify for free legal consultation from Lawyers For The Creative Arts at 312-944-ARTS (2787).

170. Learn to play an auxiliary percussion instrument.

171. "A beginner must not think about originality:
if he has it in his nature, if will come out."
— Charles Villiers Stanford,
quoted in Holst, *Holst* (1974)

172. In the beginner's mind, there are many
possibilities. In the expert's mind, there
are few.

173. "Do not take up music unless you would rather die than not do so."
 — Nadia Boulanger,
 quoted in Kendall, *The Tender Tyrant: Nadia Boulander* (1976)

174. Without R&B, there would be no rock 'n' roll.

175. Cajun and Zydeco music are not the same. Cajun music is played by the white folks living in the Acadia region of Louisiana. Zydeco music is played by the black folks living there.

176. Don't wait for success and accomplishment to find you. Go get it.

177. The number one difference between a successful person and others is not a lack of strength, not a lack of knowledge but, a lack of will.

178. "It is clear that the first specification for a composer is to be dead."
— Arthur Honegger, *I Am A Composer* (1951)

179. "I believe that an artist should be a part of his community, should work for it, and be used by it. Over the last hundred years this has become rarer, and rarer and the artist and community have both suffered as a result."
— Benjamin Britten

180. Don't underestimate the value of the Internet or "information highway" to get a record deal. There are record labels online everyday looking for new talent to sign.

181. "Music, as long as it exists, will always take its departure from the major triad and return to it. The musician cannot escape it any more than the painter his primary colours or the architect his three dimensions."
— Paul Hindemeith,
The Craft of Musical Composition (1937)

182. "Composing is a very different thing from writing tunes. Composition lives in its development."
— Leonard Bernstein,
The Joy of Music (1960)

183. Enter every contest or competition you can.

184. Always send your music to local radio stations. Many have special segments dedicated to local talent.

185.   Pay your taxes.

186.   Find an accountant you can trust.

187.   Don't forget that the tour bus is tax
       deductible. So is the gas.

188.   Call them. They won't call you.

189.   Hey, rock star! Don't forget about the band.

190. "There is one question that a composer ought always to ask of the music he is writing: Is this music that I want to hear and that otherwise I could not hear?"
— Edward Cone, quoted in Ewen, *American Composers* (1982)

191. Ration the gimmicks.

192. "You can tune a piano but you can't tune a fish."
— REO Speedwagon

193. Pure art transcends time; so does inspired music.

194. "If you want to write a bunch of songs, make a million, and be a star, you'd be better off buying lottery tickets."
— Jon Pousette–Dart,
Musician Magazine (April 1995)

195. Never burn bridges.

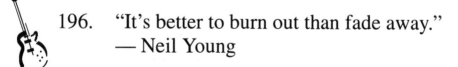

196. "It's better to burn out than fade away."
— Neil Young

197. When going on tour, don't leave town until you've confirmed with the promoter the load-in time, soundcheck time, show time, money and food arrangements – twice.

198. When on tour, make it fun. Get out and see the town. Go to a museum or the town fair.

199. When looking for musicians to join the band, look for one who moonlights as a mechanic. It could save you lots of money.

200. When planning anything, plan for the worst possible scenario. That way you'll be ready for anything.

201. Always call home when you're on tour. Believe it or not, people want to know you're still alive.

202. "Don't worry, we'll fix it in the mix."
— Heard often at recording studios around 5 A.M.

203. Work with other artists.

204. Rely on other artists.

205. Help each other.

206. Donate time to other struggling artists for mutual projects. Then every participant has something for their resume or portfolio.

207. Remember guitarists: You don't *need* that extra pedal. You *want* that extra pedal.

208. A demo tape does not need to be digitally mastered. It needs to be adequate, that's all.

209. Play every showcase you can.

210. Leave the attitude at the door. You won't make many friends with it.

211. Never forget to have fun.

212. "When performing live, don't be afraid to be silly."
      — Chicago musician

213. "Da doo doo doo, da daa daa daa."
      – The Police

214. Don't bother calling a publisher, label, agent, or club if you don't have a demo tape and PR kit to send them.

215. When touring, never identify your van for what it is.

216. When playing clubs, it's a good idea to bring your own toilet seat and toilet paper.

217. Brag when you get a chance. It's called "self–promotion."

218.   Always find out if the club has a P.A. or not.
        Otherwise, you may end up doing an
        unexpected acoustical show.

219.   Never be afraid of someone stealing your
        tunes to the extent fear inhibits your
        exposure or limits your creativity.

220. "The assumption that artists need a 'personal manager' is a persistent myth based on misinformation handed down by generations of naive, exploited musicians."
— Billy Joel,
Musician Magazine (April, 1995)

221. "Major labels are the poison in hip–hop. You can make more money selling your own tapes."
— KRS–One,
Musician Magazine (April, 1995)

222. Two of the most important words in any business or life situation are *please* and *thank–you.*

223. It never hurts to have a few good cover tunes in your repertoire.

224. It never hurts to have a few good original tunes in your repertoire.

225. In songwriting there is no secret formula. Writers write.

226. If someone offers you a record deal for a fee, they are working a scam.

227. "Nothing happens unless first a dream."
— Carl Serdling

228. Dreamers never sleep.

229. "If you can't copy others, you can't learn to create."
— Dave Roberts, Chicago musician

230. "Nothing is created, nothing is new.
      Everything is transferred."
      — Rachid Belhoucine

231. "There is no political solution to our troubled
      evolution."
      — The Police

232. "If one advances confidently in the direction of their dreams and endeavors to lead a life which they have imagined, they will meet with a success unexpected in common hours."
— Henry David Thoreau

233. "Strive for excellence and originality over image, over acceptance, over everything."
— Henry Rollins,
Musician Magazine (April, 1995)

234. Rules are meant to be broken.

235. Know the rules before you break them.

236. There are exceptions to every rule.

237. Every exception has its own rules.

238. When touring in other countries, always have local currency in hand before your arrival.

239. Be prepared to pay a "duty" charge for any goods you bring into a foreign country to sell at the gig.

240. When crossing a border into a foreign land, you have no rights. U.S. laws are not in effect.

241. Bribe a border guard and see what happens —*Go Directly To Jail. Do Not Collect $200 Dollars*.

242. No drugs or alcohol before the show. You'll end up forgetting your own lyrics or something more important.

243. Don't be afraid to handwrite text on your demo tape label. It shows honesty about the music.

244. Regarding PR kits: Send as little info as possible, but make it reflect the band's vision.

245. When touring, try and negotiate a barter with hotel management. Tell them you'll play the hotel bar for a free room or meal.

246. Get directions to the venues you are playing before you get lost.

247. "A man who has a taste of music, painting, or architecture, is like one who has another sense when compared with such as have no relish of those arts."
— Joseph Addison

248. "Sing unto the Lord with the harp; with the harp, and the voice of a psalm. With trumpets and sound of cornet make a joyful noise before the Lord, the King."
— Psalm 98:5–6

249. "Do what I do: Show up on time, play your guts out, and don't write on the walls."
— Henry Rollins,
Musician Magazine (April 1995)

250. "Whatever instrument a musician is playing, they should master the keyboard."
— Clarke Terry,
Musician Magazine (April 1995)

251. Don't be greedy. Pay your musicians fairly.

252. All studios have "downtime" they want to book. Ask your studio about downtime rates. You can usually get a better rate for these sessions.

253. Don't use your recording session as a time to practice. Know the material before you go into the studio. You'll save a lot of money.

254. Be a mentor to an aspiring artist.

255. Help people avoid the same mistakes you made.

256. "Praise Him with the sound of the trumpet; praise Him with the psaltery and harp. Praise Him with the timbrel and dance: praise Him with stringed instruments and organs."
— Psalm 150: 3–4

257. A successful songwriter may be offered a staff writer position with a large advance in exchange for splitting the publisher's share with the publisher offering the deal.

258. It is absolutely essential that a songwriter with any level of success have a good, trustworthy entertainment lawyer on his side.

259. The music publishing capitals of the world are Los Angeles, New York, and Nashville.

260. For a band or any team to be successful they must have the ability to work together toward a common vision, the ability to direct individual accomplishment toward organizational objectives. It is the fuel that allows common people to achieve uncommon feats.

261. "Remember that your instrument accompanies another, the sum of the parts makes the whole. The best bands are tribes."
— Henry Rollins,
Musician Magazine (April, 1995)

262. "Without a vision, people perish."
— Proverbs 29:18

263. Any audience is a good audience.

264. Never take yourself too seriously.

265. Very few publishers today have their own print departments. Most farm out their print work to printers who specialize in printing music.

266.   Many small publishers also farm out their legal work to an outside law firm with an entertainment law division.

267.   "I'm a revolutionary. Money means nothing to me."
– Fryderyk Chopin,
quoted in Hedley, *Chopin* (1947).

268. "Music praises God. Music is well or better able to praise Him than the building of the church and all its decoration; it is the Church's greatest ornament."
— Igor Stravinsky,
Conversation With Stravinsky (1958)

269. Stand for something or you'll fall for anything.

270. When touring, always fill up with gas after the supply drops below one–quarter of a tank.

271. Always check in with venues one or two days before the gig.

272. When you play a new town, deliver a few free tickets to local businesses. This is a great way to gain favor and fans.

273. Yesterday is but a dream, tomorrow a vision of hope. Look to this day, for it is life.

274. A mind once stretched by a new idea never regains its original dimension.

275. Critics and judges are *not* the audience.

276. "God gave me a cheerful heart, so He will surely forgive me if I serve Him cheerfully."
— Franz Joseph Haydn

277. "Nor is that musician most praiseworthy who hath longest played, but he in measured accents who hath made sweetest melody."
— William Drummond

278. Never accept a drink from a stranger when playing dates.

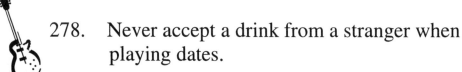

279. "I used to be a professional club musician.
Now I'm a camp counselor for adult drunks."
— Troy Neihardt, Chicago musician

280. "Life is what happens to you when you're
busy making other plans."
— John Lennon

281. Do not follow where the path may lead.
Go instead where there is no path and leave a
trail.

282.　When delivering your message, don't speak so loud they can't hear what you're saying.

283.　"The man that hath no music in himself, nor is moved with concord of sweet sounds, is fit for treason, stratagems, and spoils."
— Shakespeare

284.　"Truly there would be reason to go mad were it not for music."
— Tchaikovsky

285. "Where do I go? I go wandering in the mountains, seeking rest for my lonely heart!"
— *The Song of the Earth*

286. The key to happiness is having a dream. The key to success is making dreams come true.

287. Take risks.

288. Shit happens. Deal with it.

289.   *Music business* should be an oxymoron.

290.   Any "pseudonymous work" is a work on the copies or phonorecords of which the author is identified under a fictitious name.

291.   A copyright owner has five exclusive rights: the right to reproduce copies of the work; to prepare derivative works; to distribute those works; to perform those works; and the right to public display.

292. You don't need a lot of money or equipment to make good music.

293. There are no limits except the ones you place on yourself.

294. *Feel* the music.

295. The music industry is a bizarre business, so don't wait on others to help or discover you. Carve out your own niche and make it happen.

296.   "I feel good, I knew that I would."
         — James Brown

297.   Drugs are not musical equipment.

298.   "Works of authorship" include literary,
         musical, and dramatic works; pantomimes
         and choreographed works; pictorial, graphic,
         and sculpted works; motion pictures and
         sound recordings.

299. "Music that is born complex is not inherently better or worse than music that is born simple."
   — Aaron Copland,

300. "The melody is generally what the piece is about."
   — Aaron Copland,

301. If you have to rock the boat, make sure you know how to swim.

302.   "CHR" is an acronym for "contemporary hit radio."

303.   A "donut" is a jingle with singing at the beginning, and end and instrumental background in the middle with ad copy recorded over the middle section.

304.   The music business bible is *This Business of Music* published by Billboard Publishing. Buy it and use it.

305. "Convicts are the best audiences I ever played for."
— Johnny Cash,
Rolling Stone Magazine (1969)

306. When possible avoid all legal disputes. More times than not, they are not worth the money, time and energy.

307. Don't buy into the myth that any band you see on MTV is rich and famous.

308. Don't worry about wealth.

309. Worry about poverty.

310. Stay healthy.

311. If you're a woodwind player, try not to eat before you play.

312. The word "gig" is jargon that means "work."

313.   When done playing the harmonica always tap the mouthpiece against the palm of your hand to dislodge any saliva deposits.

314.   "Go ahead and jump."
— Van Halen, 1984

315.   The twelve modes of the major scale are: Ionian, Dorian, Phrygian, Lydian, Mixolydian, Aeolin, and Locrian.

316. Major scales are constructed of five whole steps and two half steps. The progression of which goes: W, W, H, W, W, W, H.

317. Twelve different keys exist in the realm of music. They are B, E, A, D, G, C, F, Bflat, Eflat, Aflat, Dflat, Gflat.

318. Get a business card. Next to word of mouth, it is the cheapest and easiest form of advertising around.

319. "Bed tracks" are the basic recording of each instrument on its own track or tracks before the overdubbing of other instruments and vocals.

320. We are not independent but interdependent.

321. "The grass maybe greener on the other side, but you still have to mow it."
— Dave Scott

322. "All you need is love."
— The Beatles

323. "Do what thou wilt shall be the whole of the law."
      — Aleister Crowley

324. The difference between an artist and a performer is *art*.

325. Read *All You Need Is Ears* by George Martin.

326. There are two sides to every coin. Three, if you count the edge.

327. Don't play cold. Allow yourself time to warm up before a gig.

328. Music is medicine for the soul.

329. "Music is the crystallization of sound."
— Henry David Thoreau

330. "The only reality in music is the state of mind which it induces in the listener."
— Stendhal

331. "Music is the arithmetic of sounds as optics is the geometry of light."
— Claude Debussy

332. "Music is another planet."
— Alphonse Daudet, quoted in Mencken, *Dictionary of Quotations* (1942)

333. "Music means itself."
— Eduard Hanslick, *The Beautiful in Music* (1854)

334. "Music is well said to be the speech of angels."
— Thomas Carlyle, *The Opera*

335. "Music is another lady that talks charmingly and says nothing."
— Austin O'Malley,
Keystones Of Thought (1914)

336. "Music is a safe kind of high."
— Jimi Hendrix

337. "You just pick a chord, go twang, and you've got music."
— Sid Vicious

338. "You've got to smell a lot of mule manure before you can sing like a hillbilly."
— Hank Williams

339. "The business of music should in some measure lead to the love of the beautiful."
— Plato

340. "The music is a part of us, and either
    ennobles or degrades our behavior."
    — Boethius

341. "My records are selling and I'm making
    money, but it makes me think I'm not doin'
    right."
    — Bob Dylan,
    quoted in *Life* (1964)

342. "Learning music by reading about it is like
    making love by mail."
    — Isaac Stern

343.   To sing the blues, you have to live the blues.

344.   "They laughed when I sat down at the piano.
       But when I started to play!"
       — John Caples

345. "And the night shall be filled with music,
And the cares, that infest the day,
Shall fold their tents, like the Arabs,
And as silently steal away."
— Henry Wadsworth Longfellow,
The Day Is Done

346. "When it sounds good, it IS good."
— Duke Ellington

347. "Jazz has always been a man telling the truth about himself."
— Quincy Jones

348. "Music is your own experience, your thoughts, your wisdom. If you don't live it, it won't come out of your horn."
— Charlie Parker,
quoted in Stearns, *The Story of Jazz* (1956)

349. "Folk music is the free, direct speech of the soul."
— Zoltan Kodaly, in *Nyugal*, (1918)

350. Folk music is a message from the common man.

351. "To use a woman or guitar, one must know how to tune them."
— Spanish proverb

352. "I smash a guitar because I like them. I usually smash a guitar when it's at its best."
— Pete Townshend, quoted in Green, *The Book of Rock Quotes* (1982)

353. "I frequently hear music in the heart of noise."
— George Gershwin,

354. You become successful the moment you start reaching toward your goals.

355. "Always ask for advice, but never take it."
— Gustav Host, quoted in Holst, *Holst* (1974)

356.   "You will ask where my ideas come from. I
       cannot say for certain. They come uncalled,
       sometimes independently, sometimes in
       association with other things. It seems to me
       that I could wrest them from Nature herself
       with my own hands, as I go walking in the
       woods. They come to me in the silence of
       the night or in the early morning, stirred into
       being by moods which the poet would put
       into words, but which I put into sounds; and
       these go through my head ringing and

singing and storming until at last I have them before me as notes."
— Ludwig van Beethoven,
letter to a friend (1823)

357. "A jam session is a polite endeavor—an exchange of compliments. In the old days, they had cutting contests where you defended your honour with your instrument."
— Duke Ellington

358. "Jazz came to America three hundred years ago in chains."
— Paul Whitman, *Jazz* (1926)

359. "It's taken me all my life to learn what not to play."
— Dizzy Gillespie,
quoted in Hentoff, *Jazz Is* (1978).

360. "One jazzer's jazz is another jazzer's junk."
— Ian Whitcomb, *After The Ball* (1972)

361. "I have a mistress. Lovers have come and gone, but only my mistress stays. She is beautiful and gentle. She is a swinger. She has grace. To hear her speak, you can't believe your ears. She is ten thousand year old. She is as modern as tomorrow, a brand–new woman every day, and as endless as time mathematics. Living with her is a labyrinth of ramifications. I look forward to her every gesture. Music is my mistress, and she plays second fiddle to none."
— Duke Ellington,
Music Is My Mistress (1973)

362. "All my life I was having trouble with women. Then, after I quit having trouble with them I could feel in my heart that somebody would always have trouble with them, so I kept writing those blues."
— Muddy Waters

363. "The only reason a guy learns to play an instrument is to pick up chicks."
— Billy Joel

364. "He who pays the piper calls the tune."
— English proverb

365. "Music is the only noise for which one is obliged to pay."
— Alexandre Dumas

366. "The more vulgar it is, the better they like it."
— Liberace

367. "Rock 'n' roll is instant coffee."
— Bob Geldof,
quoted in Green, *The Book Of Rock Quotes*
(1982)

368. "From time to time, play for free."
— Troy Neihardt, Chicago musician

369. When performing live, never drink more
than you can stagger offstage with.

370. "As a musician you probably won't get famous, but you'll probably get laid."
— Chicago blues musician

371. Sanity is the playground for the unimaginative.

372. "The synthesizer world opens the door to musical infinity."
— John McLaughlin, quoted in *Time* (1975)

373. Don't rely on technology. Technology is just a tool. You control it, don't let it control you.

374. "Electric guitars are an abomination. Whoever heard of an electric violin? An electric cello? Or for that matter an electric singer?"
— Andres Segovia

375. "Electrical instruments will make available for musical purposes any and all sounds that can be heard."
— John Cage

376. "Artificial instruments are not fit to be
applied to the use of disciplines."
— Aristotle

377. "I believe a composer must forge his own
forms out of the many influences that play
upon him and never close his ears to any
part of the world of sound."
— Henry Cowell

378. "Critics love mediocrity."
— Puccini

379. "Pay no attention to what the critics say; no statue has ever been put up to a critic."
— Jean Sibelius

380. "There's only two ways to sum up music: either it's good or it's bad. If it's good, you don't mess about with it; you just enjoy it."
— Louis Armstrong

381. "If the music doesn't say it, how can words say it for the music?"
— John Coltrane

382. "Music is nothing else but wild sounds
civilized into time and tune."
— Thomas Fuller

383. "Music is the art of thinking with sounds."
— Jules Combarieu

384. "Music is a beautiful opiate, if you don't
take it too seriously."
— Henry Miller

385. "Music is work."
    — John Cage

386. "Music is the best means we have of
    digesting time."
    — W.H. Auden

387. "Music has the power of producing a certain
    effect on the moral character of the soul, and
    if it has the power to do this, it is clear that
    the young must be directed to music and
    must be educated in it."
    — Unknown

388. "When I hear music, I fear no danger. I am invulnerable."
— Thoreau

389. "Music sets up a certain vibration which unquestionably results in a physical reaction. I like to think of music as an emotional science."
— Gershwin

390. "You shouldn't mess with people's heads, that's for sure. But that's what music's all about, messing with people's heads."
— Jimi Hendrix

391. "There are things known and things unknown and in between are The Doors."
— Jim Morrison

392. "Without a song the bush knife is dull."
— West African proverb.

393. "Melody is the main thing; harmony is useful only to charm the ear. "
      — Joseph Haydn

394. "Do you know that our soul is composed of harmony?"
      — Leonardo da Vinci

395. "Nowadays harmony comes almost as a shock."
      — Kathleen Raine

396. "The divine inspirations of music, poetry, and painting do not arrive at perfection by degrees, like the other sciences, but by starts, and like flashes of lightning, one here, another there, appear in various lands, then suddenly vanish."
— Pierre de Ronsard

397. Your time *will* come.

398. "Without craftsmanship, inspiration is a mere reed shaken in the wind."
— Johannes Brahms

399. "Works of art are not created; they are there, waiting to be discovered."
— Edward Elgar

400. Never make excuses. Your friends don't need them and your enemies won't believe you anyway.

401. If you want a good mix, never use a soundman with sticky fingers.

402. "The first concept is always the best and most natural. The intellect can err, the sentiment—never."
— Robert Schumann

403. "The other arts persuade us, but music takes us by surprise."
— Eduard Hanslick

404. "Never be carried away by temperament, for that dissipates strength."
— Ferruccio Busoni

405.   Whatever happens, remain calm.

406.   "You can play sharp in tune and you can play
       flat in tune."
       — Ornette Coleman

407.   "A melody is not merely something you
       can hum."
       — Aaron Copland

408.   "Art and life are not two different things."
       — Felix Mendelssohn

409. "Ever since I began to compose, I have remained true to my starting principle: not to write a page because no matter what public, or what pretty girl wanted it to be thus or thus; but to write solely as I myself thought best, and as it gave me pleasure."
— Felix Mendelssohn

410. "Melody is the very essence of music."
— Mozart

411. "The indifference of the public is what's depressing. Enthusiasm, or vehement protest, shows that your work really lives."
— Darius Milhaud

412. "Art is deaf to the demands of supply and demand."
— Ernst Bloch

413. "Music–making as a means of getting money is hell."
— Gustav Holst

414. (On his reaction to adverse criticism) "I cried all the way to the bank."
— Liberace

415. "When you get in the record business, someone gonna rip you anyway so that don't bother me. If you don't rip me, he gonna rip me, and if she don't rip me, he gonna rip me, so I'm gonna get ripped. So you don't be bothered by that because people round you gonna rip you if they can."
— Muddy Waters

416. "I pay no attention whatever to anybody's praise or blame. I simply follow my own feelings."
— Mozart

417. It is easier to understand a nation by listening to its music than by learning its language.

418. "The art of music above all other arts is the expression of the soul of the nation."
— R.V. Williams

419. "If you would know if a people are well governed, and if its laws are good or bad, examine the music it practices."
— Confucius

420. "Music is the melody whose text is the world."
— Arthur Schopenhauer

421. "Art, like charity, should begin at home.
The greatest artist belongs inevitably to
his country as much as the humblest singer
in a remote village."
— Ralph Vaughan Williams

422. "Sing unto him a new song; play skillfully
with a loud noise."
— Psalms 33:3

423. "Performance is a crucifixion."
— Charles Gained

424. "Great music is better than it can be performed."
— Arthur Schnabel

425. "It's all right letting yourself go, as long as you can let yourself back."
— Mick Jagger

426. "We shall never become musicians unless we understand the ideals of temperance, fortitude, liberality, and magnificence."
— Plato

427. "Pop music is the hamburger of every day. It is everyday life music—you can't brush your teeth to Erwartung."
— Pierre Boulez

428. "Pop music is the classical music of now."
— Paul McCartney

429. "The popular music industry has tried, repeatedly, to do with music what Ford attempts with cars. It works better with cars."
— Tony Palmer

430. "We're not interested in writing for posterity.
We just want it to sound good right now!"
— Duke Ellington

431. "If I don't practice for one day, I know it; if I
don't practice for two days, the critics know
it; if I don't practice for three days, the
audience knows it."
— Ignace Jan Paderewski

432. "I was very lucky. The people were looking for something different and I came along just in time."
— Elvis Presley

433. Creativity has a solution for any problem.

434. A solution may cause more problems.

435. "The man who has music in his soul will be most in love with the loveliest."
— Plato

436. "Music, I feel, must be emotional first and intellectual second."
— Maurice Ravel

437. "It don't mean a thing, if it ain't got that swing."
— Duke Ellington and Irving Mills

438. "I believe there can be no evolution without revolution. Why *should* we try to fit in?"
— Mick Jagger

439.   "No artist should ever marry. If you ever do
        have to marry, marry a girl who is more in
        love with your art than with you."
        — Frederick Delius

440.   "And in the end, the love you take is equal to
        the love you make."
        — Paul McCarty & John Lennon

About the Author

Scott Power is a 26 year old artist and adventurer who insists on pursuing the wildness in everything he does. Whether it's winter camping at sixty below zero, canoeing hundreds of miles down a remote river, skydiving from 13,500 feet, or backpacking through Europe, it doesn't matter. Scott sees life as an art project and won't stop until his masterpiece is finished. He has worked a variety of jobs which include fast food cook, occupational and physical therapy aid, disc-jockey, construction worker, bike messenger, musician, rock band manager, salesman, waiter, window washer, litigations clerk, painter, and farm hand. Currently, Scott is working as a free-lance writer and graphic artist. His writings have been published in three books, *Cooking The Sourdough Way, Campfire Stories Vol. 3, and Camping's Forgotten Skills,* published by ICS Books, Inc. in Merrillville, Indiana. Scott also writes a monthly column called *Online* for The Beat Magazine published by Lounge Lizard Publishing in Highland, Indiana and published on the Internet by The Times Newspapers in Hammond, Indiana. He has a Bachelor of Arts degree in Arts Management from Columbia College in Chicago. Scott resides at a former brothel in Chicago, Illinois.